EGMONT

We bring stories to life

First published in Great Britain 2020 by Egmont UK Limited,
2, Minster Court, 10th Floor, London, EC3R 7BB
www.egmont.co.uk

Text and illustrations copyright © Carolina Rabei 2020

Carolina Rabei has asserted her moral rights.

ISBN 978 1 4052 8849 1

A CIP catalogue record for this title is available from the British Library.

Stay safe online. Egmont is not responsible for content hosted by third parties.
without the prior permission of the publisher and copyright owner.

Egmont takes its responsibility to the planet and its inhabitants very seriously.
We aim to use papers from well-managed forests by responsible suppliers.

For Jom
with love
C.R.

Little Lost FOX

Carolina Rabei

Kate lived in the countryside.
There were no other children for
miles around but Kate never got lonely.
She had lots of friends to play with . . .

Miss Bunny loved stories.

Mr Ted
loved picnics.

And her very bestest favourite
of all, Ruby the Fox . . .

Wait — she was missing!

"Where's she gone?" cried Kate.

Ruby was Kate's best friend — she loved having adventures.
If she lost Ruby, Kate didn't know what she'd do!

Kate looked everywhere.
And then she saw
the pawprints . . .

So she followed and
followed them until . . .

she found a real,
live fox cub!

And the fox cub had Ruby.

"You have to give her back," said Kate. "Ruby's my friend!"

But the little cub howled when Kate tried to take Ruby.

And that's when Kate
realised something.
"You're lonely,
   aren't you?" she said.

Kate never got lonely,
but when she thought that she might,

she got a cuddle
from her mummy and
everything was all right.

That gave Kate an idea. "Ruby and I are going to help find your mummy, little cub," she said. It would be an adventure for them all!

They found a home in a tree, but when they took a peek inside, it was a squirrel mummy they saw snoozing.

They found a home by the riverside, but it was a water vole mummy who popped out and went for a swim.

They found a home by the hillside, but it was
a rabbit mummy who appeared and twitched her whiskers.

Kate looked everywhere.

And then she saw the pawprints.
They were the same shape as the little cub's,
only much, much bigger . . .
and they led into the wood.

It was cool in the wood.
There were strange noises.

Kate held on tight to Ruby
in case she felt scared.

And then she saw the eyes! Sparkling green
and watching them from the bushes.
"Be careful, little cub!" said Kate.

But the little cub knew
whose eyes they were
and he ran straight over to . . .

his mummy!

Kate watched the two of them, playing
and cuddling. The little cub and
his fox mummy were so happy.

Kate thought about her mummy. It was getting late
and she would be wondering where Kate was.

But Kate had walked for ages.
How would she ever
find her way home?

The next thing she knew, the cub
and his fox mummy were nudging
her. Getting her to follow them.

They led Kate out of the wood,
along the river and past the hillside . . .

to where her mummy was out looking for her.
"It's time for tea," said Kate's mummy, and
she gave her a great big cuddle. "Where have you been?"

"Ruby and I had an adventure," said Kate,
"and we made some new friends."

She looked around for the foxes.
They were gone, but not for long . . .

Kate had lots of friends.

Miss Bunny loved stories.
Mr Ted loved picnics.
Ruby loved adventures.
And the foxes loved spending time with Kate!